Fish on a Dish!

by Jack Tickle

Pip and Pickle are hungry,
and Percy wants his dinner!

Splash! Whoosh! Swish!
They chase that fish.

"He's hiding!" whispers Pip.
"But I'm HUNGRY!" moans Pickle.
Where could that little fish be?

"Hey, Pic
"Don't m
is getti

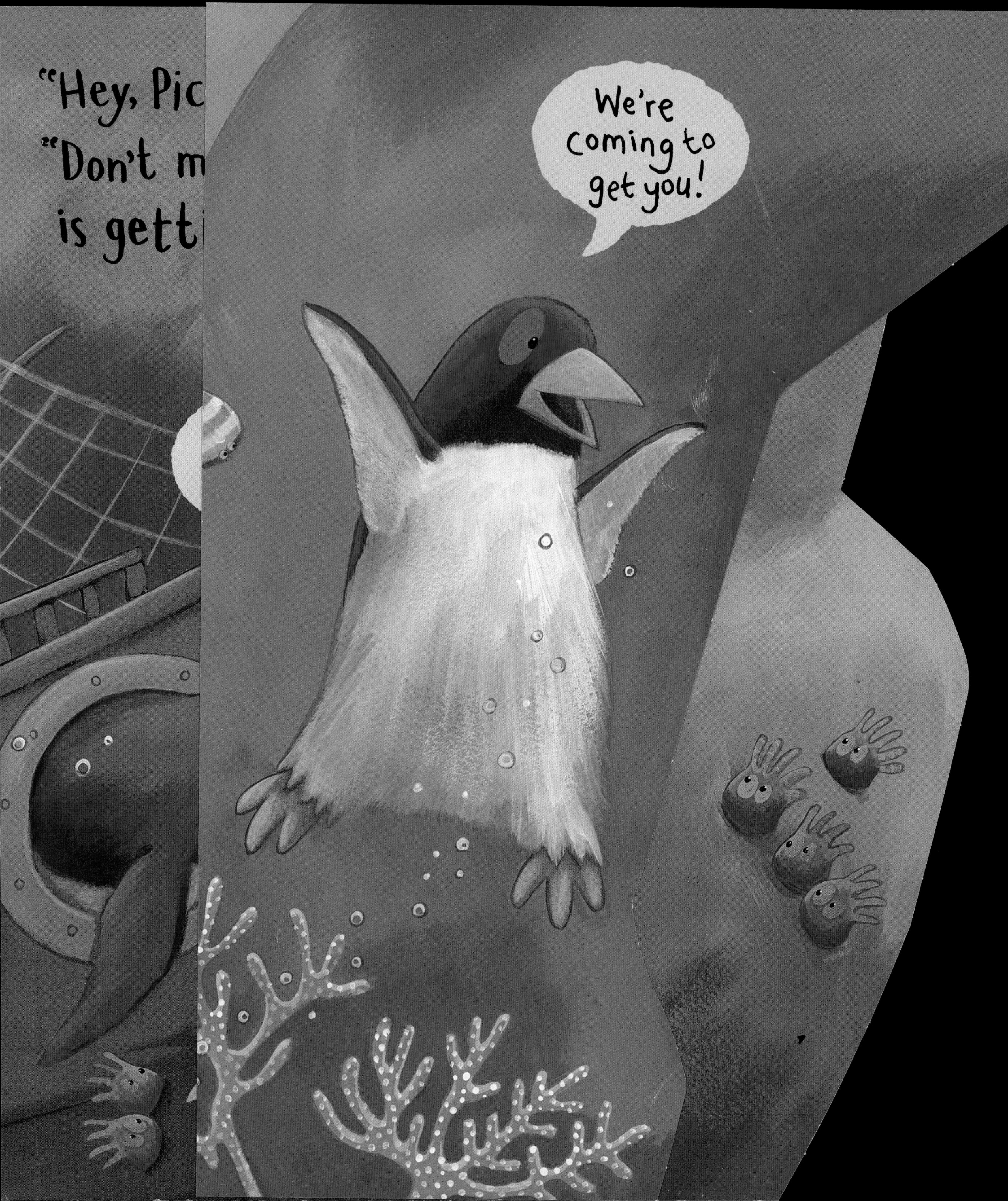

By now, the fish has found his friends.

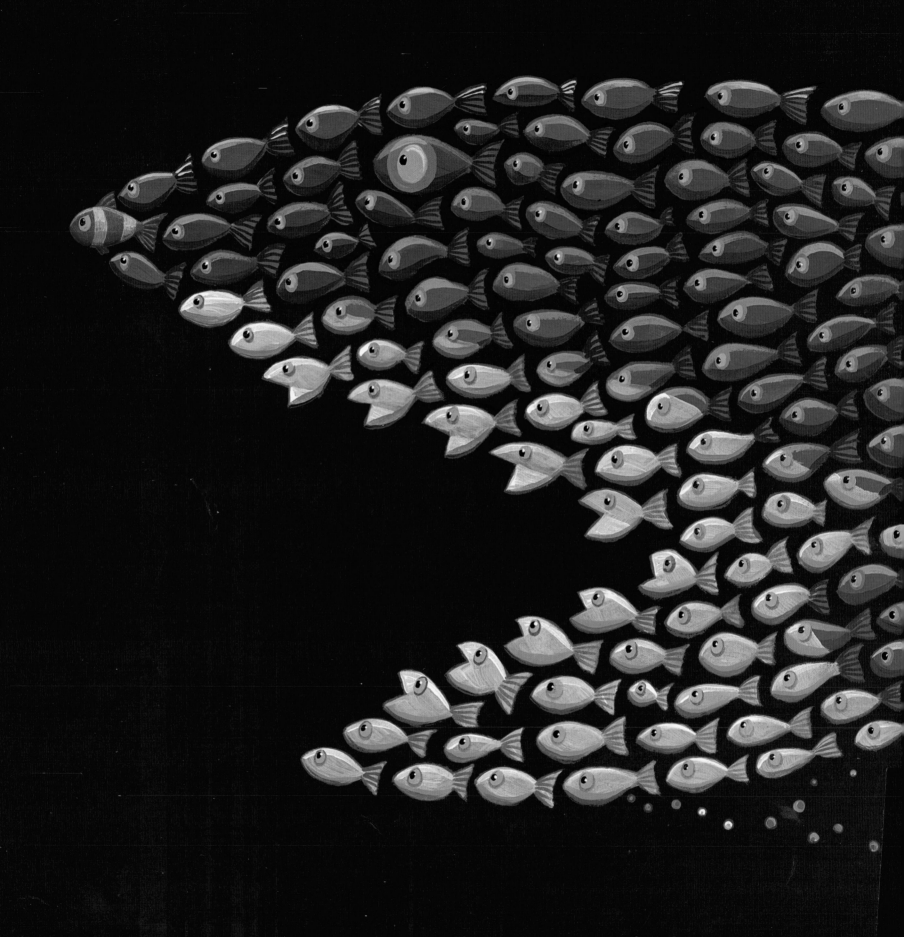

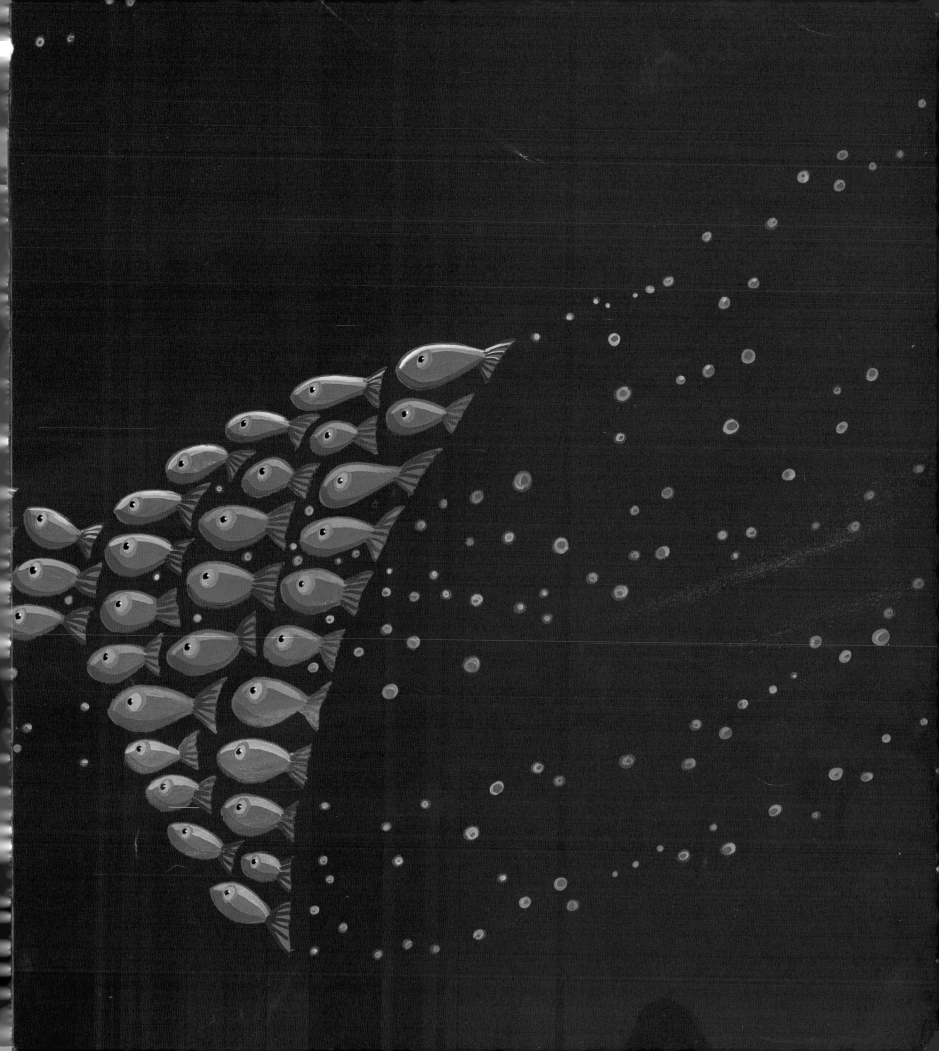

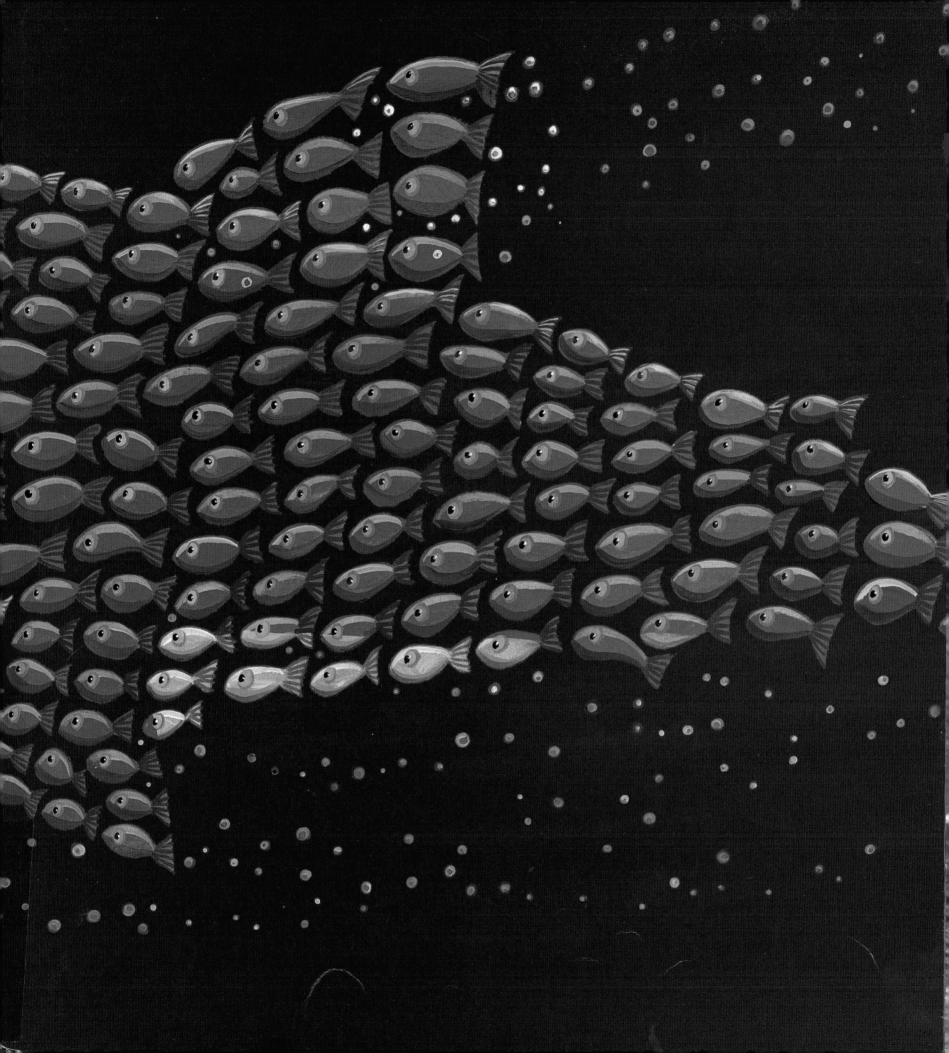

Splash! Whoosh! Swish!
Forget that fish!

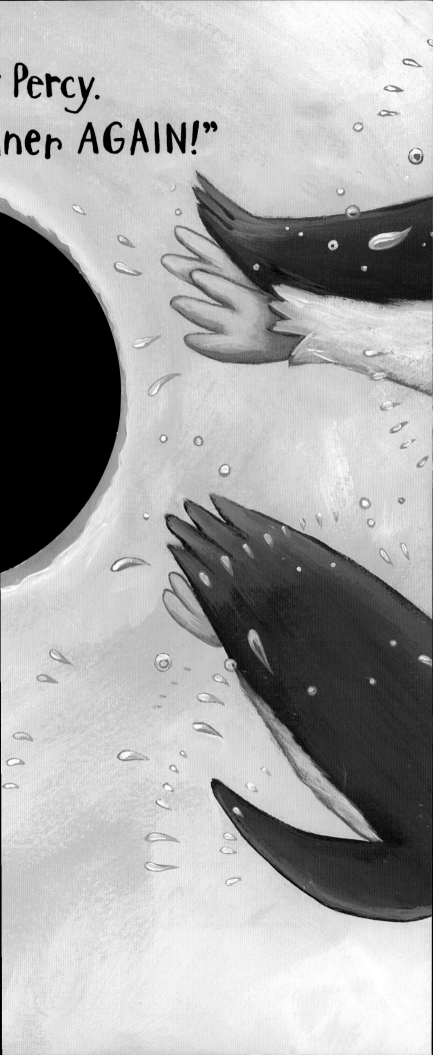